Are We There, Yeti?
ashlyn anstee
SCHOLASTIC INC.

This is Yeti.

He drives our bus.

Where are we going, Yeti?

It's a
surprise!

Are we there, Yeti?

Not yet!

YETI

Are we there, Yeti?

Not yet.

How about now?
Not yet.

Now?
Nope.
What about now?
No.

I'm hungry!
I'm bored.

I'm thirsty!
I have to go to the bathroom.
Me too!
Me three!

ARE WE YE

THERE

Yes!

This is it?

Now what?

Go have fun!

Okay, kids!
Time to go!

But we don't want to go, Yeti!
We're not tired, Yeti!
Yeah, we're not ready, Yeti!

Don't worry.
We'll come back again.

Are we home, Yeti?

To Mom and Dad,
who always answered patiently,
"Not yet!"

ISBN 978-1-338-11876-6

12 11 10 9 8 7 6 5 4 3 2 1 16 17 18 19 20 21

Printed in the U.S.A. 40

First Scholastic printing, September 2016

The text for this book is hand lettered.
The illustrations for this book are rendered using a combination of gouache and Photoshop.